DATE DUE

Treetures

Welcome Spring!

Based on the characters, art, and stories created by Judith Hope Blau

By Megan E. Bryant
Illustrated by Paul E. Nunn

Grosset & Dunlap

AMERICAN FORESTS
americanforests.org

A portion of the proceeds of the sale of this book goes to American Forests to help plant trees for forest ecosystem restoration.

Library of Congress Control Number: 2007022625

ISBN 978-0-448-44778-0   10 9 8 7 6 5 4 3 2 1

Here are the Treetures you'll meet in this book:

Twigs

Sprig

Blossom

Twigs is the Treeture Teacher. He teaches Treetures all about caring for trees and how to help them grow.

Sprig is a Treedom Fighter. He works to keep forests safe and healthy.

Blossom is a Tree Twirler. She helps the wind spread tree pollen so that baby trees can be born.

Chlorophyllis

Chlorophyll

Roothie

Rootie

Chlorophyll and Chlorophyllis are part of the Sunbeam Team. They direct sunlight to leaves so the tree can make its food and create oxygen.

Rootie and Roothie are Rooters. They care for the trees' roots and encourage them to grow.

Phloemina

Woody

Sproutlings

Mama Greenleaf

Woody and Phloemina are Sap Tappers. They care for the pipelines that bring tree food from the leaves to the roots and water from the roots to the leaves.

The Sproutlings are Twigs's class of young Treetures learning all about trees.

Mama Greenleaf is the Keeper of the Crown. She watches over the newborn leaves that grow at the tips of the branches at the top of the tree and takes care of baby Treetures.

Dear Parents and Teachers,

Do you know how important trees are to the Earth? They make oxygen for us to breathe, and they filter pollutants from the air and soil. They may even help reduce the damage of global warming. Trees are our Earth's protectors, so in return we need to protect trees. The goals of the Treetures program are to combine environmental education with entertainment and to teach children science through friendly and funny fantasy characters.

The Treetures are tiny tree keepers who live inside a big oak tree in the middle of a magical forest in a place called Nutley Grove. The family of Treetures in this book comes from enchanted acorns that grow on a very special old oak tree. The Treetures travel all over the Earth to visit other trees. When the Earth's trees are strong, other plants, wildlife, and people are healthier and happier, too. You'll meet lots of Treetures in this book. If you're ever confused about who's who, just turn to the opposite page.

After you're done reading this book, learn more about trees and the Treetures by visiting www.treetures.com.

Happy reading!

Very **TREELY** yours,

Judith Blau

Judith Hope Blau, creator

P.S. **TREE CHEERS** for you! By purchasing this book, you're helping the environment. For every book sold, I will donate a portion of my earnings to tree planting and environmental education. In addition, as part of the Treetures publishing program, Grosset & Dunlap will donate money to American Forests, a nonprofit organization that helps plant trees for forest ecosystem restoration.

TWIGS'S GUIDE TO THE PARTS OF A TREE!

LEAF

BLOSSOM

BUD

BRANCH

PHLOEM

CROWN

XYLEM

TRUNK

ROOTS

Hi, kids!

I'm Twigs, the Treeture Teacher. The Treetures are magical creatures who live inside a big oak tree in the middle of an enchanted forest in a place called Nutley Grove. The Treetures care for trees all around the world. They teach kids like you about trees and how to care for them and the environment. In this book you'll be learning about the parts of a wild apple tree. If you ever get confused, you can always turn back to this picture for help.

GLOSSARY

BLOSSOM: a flower that can be found on some trees in the springtime.

BRANCH: a branch extends from the trunk of a tree.

BUD: a blossom or a leaf that hasn't bloomed yet.

CARBON DIOXIDE (say it like: **car**-bun dye-**ox**-ide): a gas in the air that trees take in to help make their food.

CHLOROPHYLL (say it like: **klohr**-uh-fil): the substance in leaves that gives them their green color.

CROWN: the top of a tree where the branches, twigs, and leaves grow.

LEAF: a leaf grows from a branch or a twig.

NECTAR (say it like: **neck**-tur): a sweet liquid inside a tree flower that attracts birds and bees to the flower.

NUTRIENTS: vitamins, minerals, and other substances that trees need in order to grow healthy and strong.

OXYGEN (say it like: **ox**-ih-jen): leaves release oxygen that animals and humans breathe in.

PHLOEM (say it like: **flow**-um): phloem vessels are like pipes that carry sap from the leaves to the rest of the tree.

PHOTOSYNTHESIS (say it like: foh-toh-**sin**-thuh-sis): the process of sunlight mixing with carbon dioxide and water so that a tree can make its food and release oxygen.

POLLEN: a sticky or powdery yellow substance found in blossoms.

POLLINATION (say it like: pol-ih-**nay**-shun): the process of pollen traveling from one blossom to another.

ROOTS: the roots hold the tree in the ground and bring water from the ground into the trunk of the tree.

SAP: a sticky fluid that trees use as food.

STOMATA (say it like: stoh-**mah**-tuh): tiny openings on the underside of many leaves through which a tree takes in carbon dioxide and releases oxygen and moisture.

TRUNK: the bark-covered middle of the tree that connects the roots at the bottom to the crown at the top.

VESSELS: long pipes through which water and sap flow up and down the tree.

XYLEM (say it like: **zy**-lum): the xylem vessels are like pipes that carry the water from the roots up to the rest of the tree.

ROOT-A-MENTARY ELEMENTARY SCHOOL

Mama Greenleaf and Twigs get the Sproutlings ready for school.

WELCOME TO NUTLEY GROVE

Once upon a late winter's day, Nutley Grove was quiet and still. The forest seemed fast asleep—but not inside the Great Oak. Even though there was snow on the ground, the Treetures were getting ready for spring!

Ready to plant!

Ready for sap tapping!

Ready for rooting!

Ready for tree twirling!

3

Twigs, the Treeture Teacher, called together his new class of Sproutlings. "Welcome to Root-a-Mentary Elementary School!" he announced. "We'll be learning all about trees. Trees are very important to everything that lives in Nutley Grove. Does anyone know why?"

One of the Sproutlings raised his hand. "Because they're so big?"

Can you think of other reasons why trees are so important?

4

"Very good," said Twigs. "Because they're big, trees provide shade for the animals on hot summer days. But there are also many other reasons why trees are one of nature's treasures, and we'll be learning all of them."

They all cheered, except for one. "Where did you get that?" she asked Twigs, pointing to the green heart on his overalls.

Twigs smiled. "I earned this when I was a Sproutling just like the three of you. But before you can earn your green heart, you must learn all about the parts of a tree."

"I sure hope I get my green heart soon," said one Sproutling.

"You will," said Twigs. "Once you are done with my lessons."

Early the next morning, Twigs led the Sproutlings through the snow-covered forest. "The trees might be bare, but they are alive and well, even during the coldest days of winter," he explained. "It's the Treetures' job to take care of them. Do you see that tree up ahead? That tree is the youngest apple tree in Nutley Grove and this is its first apple-making year. If we take extra-good care of it now, there will be apples in the fall for all the woodland creatures to eat!"

The Sproutlings ran up to the apple tree. "How do we take care of it?" asked one.

"First, let's inspect the tree," Twigs said. "It has nice strong branches, and fallen leaves are covering the ground over the roots. Very good, but let's add more fallen leaves to the base of the tree."

"Why?" a little Sproutling asked.

"The leaves will protect the roots from freezing in the cold snow, and later the leaves will decay and turn into rich soil that helps the tree grow," replied Twigs.

Within a few weeks, the first signs of spring could be seen all over Nutley Grove! The snow and ice were melting, the breeze was soft, and there were many gentle rain showers. And when it wasn't raining, the sun was getting warmer every day.

On one bright and sunny day, the Sproutlings went on another field trip with Twigs, where they met a Treeture named Sprig. "Hi, Sproutlings. I'm a Treedom Fighter," Sprig introduced himself. "It's the job of every Treedom Fighter to keep the forest healthy."

"What can we do to help, Sprig?" asked a Sproutling.

"We need to make signs so that everyone knows that it's time to welcome spring and to be careful in the forest," explained Sprig. "You see, the forest will soon be full of new plants and flowers, and that new growth is very delicate. A little tender loving care from us will keep it safe! Now let's get to work!"

Sprig, Twigs, and the Sproutlings placed signs all over Nutley Grove, sticking them in the ground, painting them on rocks, and hanging them on the tree branches (instead of nailing them to the bark, of course)!

TREE CHEERS FOR TREES

A few days later, Twigs brought the Sproutlings back to the apple tree. There they met Rootie and Roothie!

"Hey, Sproutlings!" Roothie exclaimed. "Who's ready to learn about *roots*?"

"Me! Me! Me!" sang the Sproutlings.

"We're the Rooters. It's our job to care for the tree's roots," explained Rootie. "The roots hold the tree in the ground, store tree food, and bring water from the ground to the trunk of the tree. Without the roots, the trees would be very thirsty. We don't want that to happen, so we help the water move up the roots and into the tree trunk."

"The water is full of nutrients. Nutrients are full of vitamins and minerals which the tree needs to grow, grow, grow!" Roothie continued.

"That reminds me of our special cheer," Rootie said. "It goes like this: Grow, Tree, Grow!"

"Everybody ready?" asked Roothie. "One, two, three . . ."

"Grow, Tree, GROW!" cheered the Sproutlings.

ROOT, ROOT, ROOT!

Have you rooted for your favorite tree today? You can be a Rooter just like Rootie and Roothie. All you have to do is cheer on the trees in your neighborhood by telling them, "Grow, Tree, Grow!" Just follow this cheer with your friends!

TRUNK EXPLORERS

For their next lesson, the Sproutlings had to wear helmets and boots. They were going into the trunk of the apple tree with Woody and Phloemina.

"We're the Sap Tappers," Phloemina said. "We make sure the tree gets enough food and water."

"First stop is the *xylem vessels*," Woody said. "The xylem is the part of the trunk that carries the water from the roots to the rest of the tree. It's like a bunch of pipes or straws. I listen to the xylem to make sure every part of the tree gets water."

Xylem in Action!

You can watch xylem in action, right in your very own home. Before you try this fun experiment, make sure you get an adult's permission.

Supplies

- Tall, clear drinking glass or glass jar
- Red or blue food coloring
- Spoon and knife
- 1 carnation or celery stalk

1. Add enough water to the glass or jar so that it is 3/4 full.

2. Next, add several drops of food coloring, enough so that the water in the glass turns a deep, vibrant color. Stir so that it is completely mixed.

3. Have an adult use the knife to cut off the bottom of the carnation stem or celery stalk.

4. Place the carnation or celery stalk in the glass. The thirsty plant will drink the water. By the next day, you'll see colored streaks spread through the flower's or stalk's xylem!

"If you look over there, you'll see another layer of the trunk that's full of pipes—the *phloem vessels*," Phloemina said. "The phloem carries *sap*—a sticky, sugary substance that trees use as food—from the leaves to the rest of the tree. By checking on the phloem, I can make sure the tree is getting all the food it needs."

The Sproutlings looked happy to be learning so much but they couldn't help wondering if their green hearts would appear now that they knew all about xylem and phloem.

THE CROWN AT THE TOP OF THE TREE

"Hello, my dears," said Mama Greenleaf when the Sproutlings arrived at the *crown*. "I hope you've learned lots from our super Sap Tappers."

"We did, Mama Greenleaf!" cried the Sproutlings excitedly.

"Come, let's take a peek at the newborn leaves!" Mama Greenleaf said.

"The crown of the tree is made up of all the tree's twigs and branches," Mama Greenleaf continued. "And out of those branches grow leaves."

"They're so soft!" whispered one Sproutling.

"I'm here to care for these baby leaves," Mama Greenleaf said.

"Now who can tell me what *this* is?" Mama Greenleaf continued, pointing to something small and round.

"Is it—is it a baby *bud*?" asked a Sproutling.

"Exactly right!" Mama Greenleaf said with pride. "Soon these buds will open and become beautiful blossoms."

From the Soup to Nuts Kitchen
Branch Toast

The Treetures love to eat Mama Greenleaf's special Branch Toast! Her recipe uses two delicious gifts from trees: cinnamon and maple syrup. Always have an adult help when you make this yummy recipe. When you see this symbol ⓘ, it means that an adult should do this step.

Serves 4; 1 slice of Branch Toast per person

Ingredients

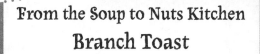

2 eggs
1/2 cup milk
1/4 tsp cinnamon
1/2 tbs butter
4 slices bread
1 cup maple syrup

1. Whisk together the eggs, milk, and cinnamon. Pour the mixture into a shallow baking dish or pan.

ⓘ 2. Melt the butter in a large frying pan over medium heat.

3. Meanwhile, dip each slice of bread into the egg mixture so that both sides are coated.

ⓘ 4. Fry the bread in the frying pan, turning once, so that both sides are golden brown. Add more butter to the pan if necessary.

5. Serve each piece of Branch Toast with 1/4 cup warm maple syrup. What a "treet"!

"I know Twigs told you that trees are very important," Mama Greenleaf said to the Sproutlings. "But do you know why?"

"There are lots of reasons," answered a Sproutling.

"That's right!" said Mama Greenleaf. "Twigs has a special list all about the gifts of trees. Let's all read it!"

The Sproutlings soon finished reading Twigs's list.

"Wow!" a Sproutling exclaimed. "Trees give us so much."

"Mama Greenleaf?" a Sproutling asked, looking down at his overalls. "Now that we know all about the gifts of trees, where are our green hearts?"

THE GIFTS OF TREES

Trees give us food and nuts to eat.
Thank you, trees, for such a special treat!

Trees give us shade and
a cool place to rest.
They make homes for animals
and birds to nest.

Trees give us wood for homes
in each city and town.
Please don't forget to replace
the trees we cut down.

Trees hold the soil in its place
night and day
So our precious Earth won't wash away!

Trees shield our homes from
summer's sunshine
and protect us from the
winds of frosty wintertime!

Trees clean our air—a present so rare.

Trees give us oxygen to breathe.
What a wonderful gift to receive!

Mama Greenleaf smiled. "Be patient, Sproutlings. There is still more you need to learn. But don't worry, you'll earn your green hearts soon enough."

"Now, there is a gas in the air called *carbon dioxide*. Leaves take in carbon dioxide through tiny openings called *stomata*. Carbon dioxide warms the Earth, so by taking it in trees help to cool the Earth. Trees also release *oxygen* and moisture through the stomata. The oxygen gives us fresh air to breathe!"

Some of the Sproutlings were puzzled. "I don't understand, Mama Greenleaf," one of them said. "How does *all that* happen? Tell us again!"

"I think it's time you heard from Chlorophyll and Chlorophyllis!" Mama Greenleaf said.

STOMATA

17

THE SUNBEAM TEAM

TREE FOOD RECIPE

1. Lots of sunshine

2. Just enough carbon dioxide from the air

3. Water and nutrients from the roots

4. Blend together and tree food is made!

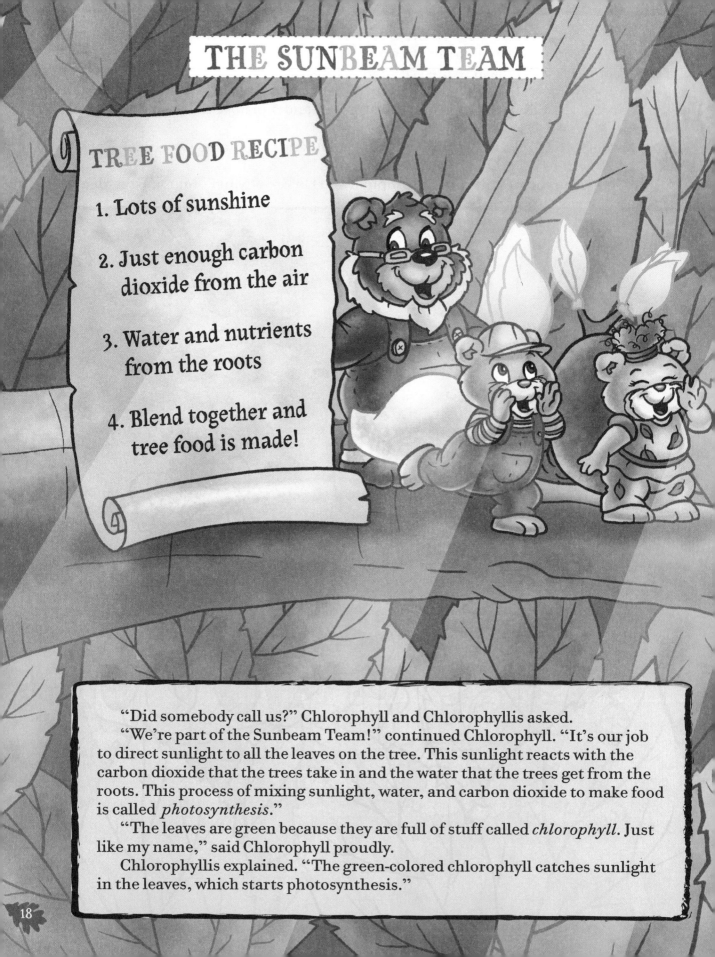

"Did somebody call us?" Chlorophyll and Chlorophyllis asked.

"We're part of the Sunbeam Team!" continued Chlorophyll. "It's our job to direct sunlight to all the leaves on the tree. This sunlight reacts with the carbon dioxide that the trees take in and the water that the trees get from the roots. This process of mixing sunlight, water, and carbon dioxide to make food is called *photosynthesis*."

"The leaves are green because they are full of stuff called *chlorophyll*. Just like my name," said Chlorophyll proudly.

Chlorophyllis explained. "The green-colored chlorophyll catches sunlight in the leaves, which starts photosynthesis."

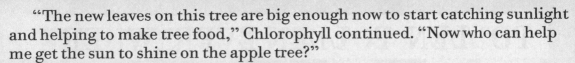

"The new leaves on this tree are big enough now to start catching sunlight and helping to make tree food," Chlorophyll continued. "Now who can help me get the sun to shine on the apple tree?"

"Me! Me! Me!" exclaimed the Sproutlings.

"Okay, everybody!" Chlorophyllis said. "Cup your hands around your mouth and yell, 'Over here, sun! Shine, shine, shine!'"

"OVER HERE, SUN! SHINE, SHINE, SHINE!" they shouted.

Suddenly, everything around them seemed brighter! The spring sun was shining directly onto the young apple tree. And even though they couldn't see it happening, the Sproutlings knew that the tree was making food and putting oxygen into the air.

A few days later, the Sproutlings returned to the crown of the apple tree. Spring had taken over Nutley Grove—flowers were blooming, bees were buzzing, and birds were chirping!

"The buds have opened!" exclaimed a Sproutling. "Look at all the *blossoms*!"

POLLEN

STAMEN

POLLEN TUBE

EGGS

PETAL

STEM

LEAF

"Hello, everyone!" trilled a voice. "My name is Blossom, and I'm a Tree Twirler! I help spread *pollen* so that baby trees can be born."

"When the blossoms open, a yellow substance called pollen is revealed," Blossom explained. "Then the pollen from one blossom travels to another blossom so it can join with teeny-tiny eggs to become a seed! This is called *pollination*. Isn't that amazing?"

One Sproutling raised her hand. "But Blossom, how do flowers share their pollen?"

"There's a sweet liquid inside the flower called *nectar*. Birds and bees love to drink it, and when they do, pollen gets stuck to their bodies. Then, when birds and bees visit other blossoms, they carry the pollen with them," Blossom said.

"Wind also helps spread pollen," Blossom continued. "I have a special dance to help the wind spread pollen."

"Teach it to us!" cried the Sproutlings.

Blossom and the Sproutlings danced along the crown of the tree until they were too tired to dance anymore.

"Beautiful job, Sproutlings!" Blossom said sweetly. "Now you're ready for the Pollination Celebration—a magical day when all the Treetures help the wind spread pollen by dancing!"

Welcome Spring!

How do you and your friends and family celebrate the beautiful, warm days of spring?

Once the Sproutlings learned about the Pollination Celebration, they couldn't wait for it to come! They passed the warm spring days by helping Sprig, Rootie, Roothie, Woody, Phloemina, Mama Greenleaf, Chlorophyll, Chlorophyllis, and Blossom whenever they needed a hand.

At last, the day of the Pollination Celebration arrived! In a large clearing in the middle of Nutley Grove, not far from the apple tree, all the Treetures gathered to dance with Blossom and help spread the pollen.

All the Treetures twirled around and a warm spring breeze spread the pollen from the apple tree's blossoms all over Nutley Grove. "Happy spring, Treetures!" Twigs announced.

SUMMER SMILES

A few weeks later, Twigs and Mama Greenleaf heard one of the Sproutlings crying. They rushed to the apple tree, where the Sproutlings had gathered.

"All the blossoms are gone!" cried the Sproutlings.

"Don't worry," Twigs said. "Each blossom's petals fall off the tree by the time spring ends. These petals turn into vitamins for the soil!"

"Remember the Pollination Celebration?" Mama Greenleaf asked. "The pollen and eggs created seeds inside the apple tree's blossoms. By the fall, these seeds will turn into apples."

Suddenly, Mama Greenleaf pointed to the Sproutlings' overalls. "Look!" she exclaimed. "Your green hearts have appeared."

The Sproutlings looked down and saw what they'd been waiting for all spring—their green hearts!

"Wow!" exclaimed the Sproutlings. "That's so cool!"

"I can't wait to be a Tree Twirler when I grow up," a Sproutling said.

"I'm going to be a Sap Tapper!" said another.

"You're going to make tree-mendous Treetures, Sproutlings," Twigs said.

The Sproutlings giggled and beamed almost as brightly as the sun!

What Can I Do to Earn My Green Heart?

The Sproutlings' green hearts appeared once they learned all about the parts of a tree and how important trees are to the Earth. You can earn a green heart, too. It won't appear magically on your clothes, but if you do the things on this list, you'll know that your heart is green on the inside. Saying that your heart is green on the inside means that you care about trees and the Earth.

Always get permission to help care for a tree in your yard or neighborhood.

♥ During hot and dry spells, water the trees in your yard. Water slowly.

♥ Gently loosen the soil around the trunk of a tree. This will allow air and water to reach the roots.

♥ Plant flowers around the base of a tree trunk. They will tell you if the tree needs water.

♥ Be sure your pets do not hurt trees. Do not let their waste burn tree roots.

♥ Do not place signs or decorations on trees that might damage bark or break branches.

♥ Report a cracked branch or tree trunk to someone who can call an arborist, or tree doctor. Even trees need a checkup sometimes!

♥ Report holes or decay in or on a tree. The tree may be sick from fungus or harmful insects.

♥ Watch the trees in your neighborhood change with each season.

♥ Most of all, enjoy the shade and beauty of the trees around you.